New Kid in Town

New Kid in Town

Written and Illustrated by
Charles Robinson

Atheneum 1975 *New York*

Library of Congress Cataloging in Publication Data

Robinson, Charles,
New kid in town.

SUMMARY: The new boy in town meets the challenges of
his neighbor but gets the worst of it until he learns to
use the situations to his own advantage.

I.   Title.
PZ7.R5653Ne   [E]   75-8870
ISBN 0-689-30484-6

To Cynthia

Are you the new kid?
Come on over—

We'll build a tree fort. I'll
take the tools, you bring the wood.

I'll do the hammering. You hold it steady.

We'll have a garden. You
dig. I'll plant the seeds.

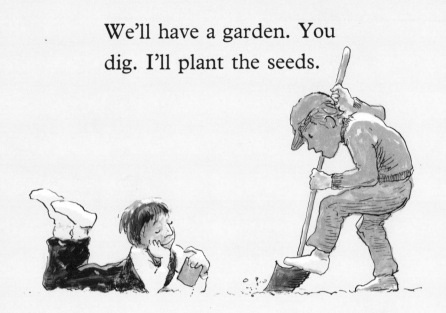

Can't you make straighter rows?

I'll be a robber, you're the victim.

The victims burned up! Lucky I'm a fireman.

I'm a doctor, you're the patient.

You're very sick. Ten dollars please.

I'm a bull, you're the bullfighter.

I'm a tow truck, you're the wreck.

I'm a bulldozer. You're in my way.

I don't want to play anymore.

...mean! Bully!

My, he's not a very good driver, is he?

You wouldn't cry like that!

I don't think he's so great!

She's right!

That Night

Next Day

Hey, I've got some more games for you!

I'm the cowboy, you're the horse.

Whoops, sorry! Horsie went out of control.

I'm an astronaut. You can be ground control.

Blast Off!

I'm a hunter, you'd better hide.
You're an animal.

Grrrrrrr!

I'm a trapeeze artist. You hold that rope tight.

Oops! The rope slipped.

I'm a King. Bring me a root beer.

Sorry, Your Majesty.

I'm a terrific track star. You cheer
when I come over the finish line.

Hooray!

Hey, cut it out!

No!

Say, do you like checkers?